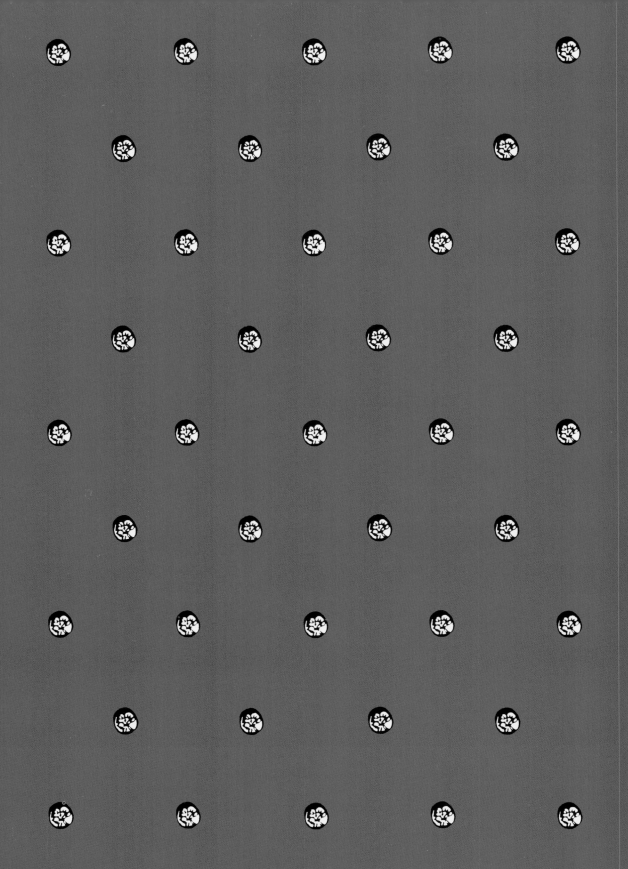

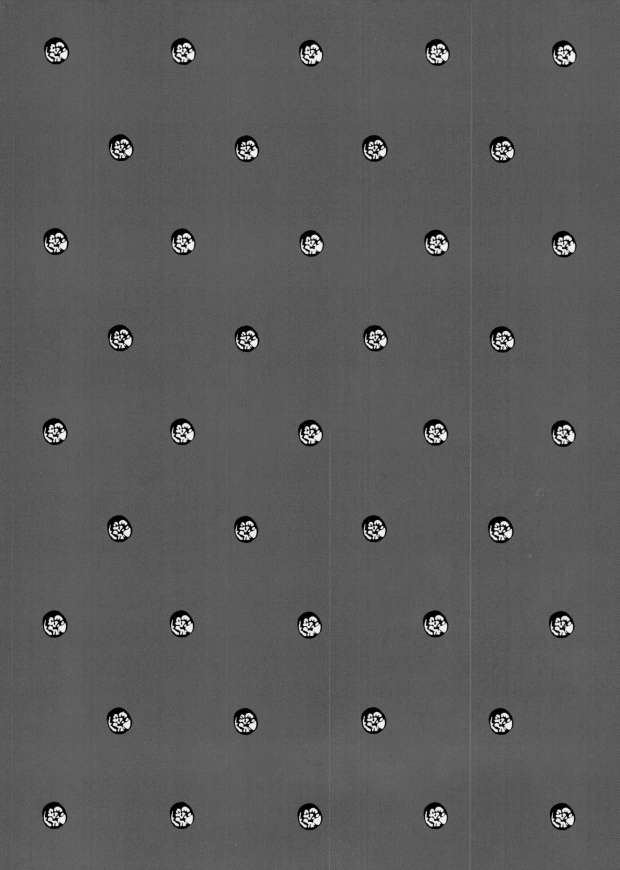

Tết the New Year

SIMON & SCHUSTER BOOKS FOR YOUNG READERS
Published by Simon & Schuster
New York London Toronto Sydney Tokyo Singapore

SIMON & SCHUSTER BOOKS FOR YOUNG READERS

Simon & Schuster Building, Rockefeller Center, 1230 Avenue of the Americas, New York, New York 10020

Copyright © 1992 by The Children's Museum, Boston. First SIMON & SCHUSTER BOOKS FOR YOUNG READERS edition 1993. Originally published by Modern Curriculum Press as part of the Multicultural Celebrations created under the auspices of The Children's Museum, Boston. Leslie Swartz, Director of Teacher Services, organized and directed this project with funding from The Hitachi Foundation. All rights reserved including the right of reproduction in whole or in part in any form. Photographs: 2, Hong Kong Tourist Association; 9, 10, 14, Leslie Swartz; 12, Mai Vo-Dinh. SIMON & SCHUSTER BOOKS FOR YOUNG READERS is a trademark of Simon & Schuster. Manufactured in Mexico.

10 9 8 7 6 5 4 3 2   ISBN: 0-671-79843-x

Huy Ly was in a hurry. He was afraid he would be late for his English language class. If only he didn't have so much on his mind.

"Good morning, Huy," Ms. Kim said as he took his seat. "Since it's January, we were talking about *Têt.* Mai was about to tell us her favorite part of the Vietnamese New Year."

1

"My whole family got together on New Year's Eve in Việt Nam. I stayed up after midnight to make the sweet rice cakes and we all lighted firecrackers! That's what I liked best," Mai said.

Then Tân raised his hand. "Here in the United States, my family goes to the *Tết* celebration at the high school. They have all the special foods and a dragon dance and everything. Last year my brother was the dragon's tail!"

"Wait—I changed my mind," interrupted Mai. "I forgot about the red envelopes of money that we got at *Tết*. That's what I liked best."

2

"I know the part of *Tết* I DON'T like," said Hùng. "My mother says I have to be nice to everyone— even my little brother."

Ms. Kim turned to Huy and asked, "What about you, Huy? What do you like best about celebrating *Tết*?" Huy shook his head and looked down. He didn't want to think about *Tết*. It made him miss his mother and everyone in Việt Nam they had left behind. It made him worry about his father who was so lonely and so lost in the new country.

Huy finally answered, "My father says we don't celebrate *Tết* here. He says 'No country— no New Year.'"

Linh joined in. "Yes, my parents always say *Tết* isn't the same here. But I remember very little about it. I wonder what *Tết* was like in Việt Nam."

5

"Me too," exclaimed the other children.

"Then the best way to find out is to have our own *Tết* celebration," said Ms. Kim. "On Saturday, let's meet at noon at Liên Nhủ's Market to buy the supplies. Then we can go to my apartment and celebrate the New Year."

All the children were excited—all except Huy. He didn't feel much like celebrating anything. His new year wasn't looking too happy. As he walked home by himself, he heard Tân calling behind him.

"Huy, let's walk home together. My mom made candied ginger for Ms. Kim. Even though it's a special gift for our teacher, I don't think she'd mind if we had a taste."

"No thanks," Huy answered.

6

"Are you coming on Saturday then?"

"No. I don't want to. Besides, my father doesn't go to work that day. I should be at home."

"Well, if you change your mind, I'll be waiting for you in front of my apartment," Tân answered.

Saturday came and Tân waited for Huy, but Huy did not show up.

"Tân, you made it," said Ms. Kim when he arrived at the market out of breath. "We'd better get on with our shopping."

Ms. Kim gave everyone a job. "Tân, please look for sweet rice and *mung beans* to make rice cakes. Mai, you find some coconut milk, dried watermelon seeds, and candied fruit. Linh, you look for two red candles, three small teacups, and incense. Hùng, you choose two nice grapefruit, some mangoes, and a big papaya. I'll get the noodles and the *bông mai*—the plum blossoms. Then we'll go to the butcher's for the pork, and some duck for the soup."

When they arrived at Ms. Kim's she said, "I've cleaned this place from top to bottom for *Tết* as I would in Việt Nam! Did you all know that is an important New Year's custom?"

"What are those red strips of paper with writing on them?" Linh asked.

"Those are *câu dôi*—poems written about the yearning for home and family," Ms. Kim answered. "Now, let's set up the altar on this table."

Ms. Kim put a picture of her grandfather in the middle of the altar. Then she placed a *bài vi*, a piece of wood showing his name, below it with some coins.

"Hùng, put fruit next to the coins, please. That means our ancestors will have the things they will need in their life after death."

12

"I know about the candles," said Mai. "They stand for the sun and moon, and the incense stands for the stars."

"And I remember the part about praying in front of the altar at midnight," interrupted Linh. "We pray for a good year and good health for our family and friends. Right, Ms. Kim?"

"Right, Linh. And we visit those friends on the third day of the celebration. That's the day after you have invited your teacher for a big dinner!" she said laughing.

"This would be a perfect third day of *Tết* if all our friends were here," said Tân. "I wish Huy had come."

14

"Well, it's hard for Huy. This is his first *Tết* away from Việt Nam. Some of you know what it feels like to be a stranger in a new country," she said.

"But he isn't a stranger! He is our friend!" exclaimed Tân.

"Wait, I have an idea," Ms. Kim said. "I think I will give Huy's father a call to invite them to join us. They don't live very far from here, do they?"

Ms. Kim phoned Huy's father and convinced him to come with his son for the celebration.

Tân was so pleased that he quickly put on his coat and ran to Huy's apartment. Huy's father answered the door.

"Happy New Year, Mr. Ly! I'm so happy that you and Huy are coming to our *Tết* celebration," Tân said breathlessly.

When Mr. Ly, Huy, and Tân arrived at Ms. Kim's apartment, she opened the door with a smile. *"Chúc Mùng Nam Mói,"* she said to them. "Good wishes to you for the New Year." Then she opened the door wider.

Behind her, Huy and his father could see the beautiful *Tết* altar, the table laid with a New Year's feast, and around it a circle of grinning faces. Huy saw his father's look of surprise turn into a shy smile.

"Please come in and join us," said Ms. Kim. "Friends should be with friends at *Tết*. We will all be together to celebrate a new beginning for a New Year."

And so they were.

20

Glossary

bài vi (BYE VEE) a piece of wood showing the name of a person who has died

bông mai (BAHNG MY) plum blossoms

câu dôi (KOW DOY) poems written about the yearning for home and family

Chúc Mùng Nam Mói (CHOOK MUNG NAHM MOY) Happy New Year!

Hùng (HUNG) boy's name

Huy (HOO-oy) boy's name

Liên Nhù (LEE-an NOO) grocery owner's name

Linh (LIN) girl's name

Ly (LEE) family name

Mai (MY) girl's name

mung beans (MUNG BEENS) small green beans for cooking and growing bean sprouts

Tân (TUHN) boy's name

Têt (TET) Vietnamese New Year

About the Author

Kim-Lan Tran is a noted Vietnamese writer. She grew up in Saigon, Việt Nam, and first came to the United States in 1968 as a student. She returned to her homeland where she taught English for many years. With a Master's Degree in English as a Second Language, Ms. Tran teaches in the bilingual program at Edison Middle School in Boston.

About the Illustrator

Mai Vo-Dinh was born and raised in Hué, Việt Nam. He studied at the Lycée of Hué, and at the Sorbonne, the Académie de la Grande Chaumière, and the Ecole Nationale Supérieure des Beaux-Arts in Paris. His work has been exhibited throughout the United States, Canada, Europe, and Việt Nam, and has appeared on UNICEF greeting cards. Mr. Vo-Dinh has illustrated a multitude of books, including the award-winning *First Snow* written by his wife, Helen Coutant. He and his wife reside in Maryland with their two daughters, Phuong-Nam and Linh-Giang.

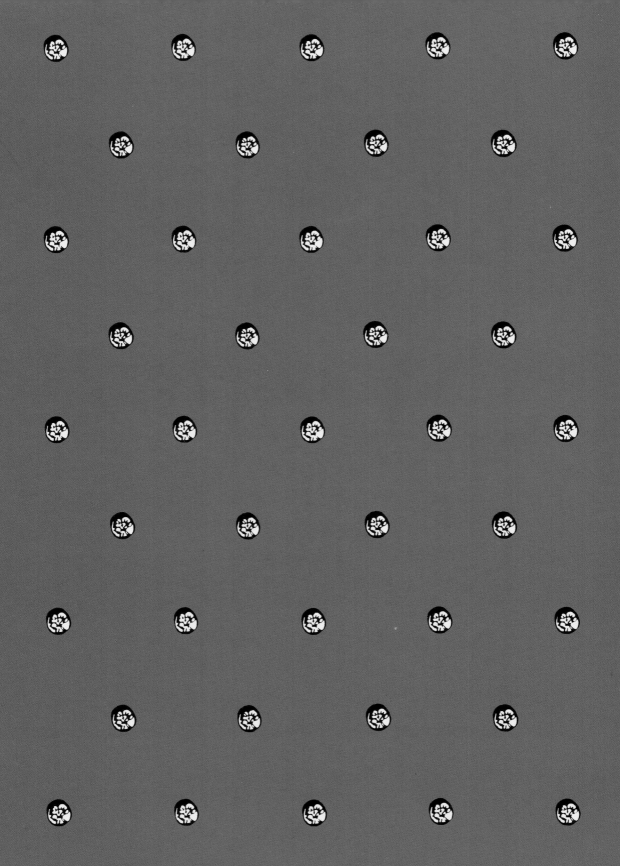